D0522109

CAT'S WITCH
AND THE
MONSTER

TIGER series

Damon Burnard	*Revenge of the Killer Vegetables*
Lindsay Camp	*Cabbages from Outer Space*
Mick Fitzmaurice	*Morris Macmillipede*
Elizabeth Hawkins	*Henry's Most Unusual Birthday*
Kara May	*Cat's Witch* *Cat's Witch and the Lost Birthday* *Cat's Witch and the Monster* *Cat's Witch and the Wizard* *Tracey-Ann and the Buffalo*
Barbara Mitchelhill	*The Great Blackpool Sneezing Attack*
Penny Speller	*I Want to be on TV*
Robert Swindells	*Rolf and Rosie*
John Talbot	*Stanley Makes It Big*
Joan Tate	*Dad's Camel*
Hazel Townson	*Amos Shrike, the School Ghost* *Blue Magic* *Snakes Alive!* *Through the Witch's Window*
Jean Wills	*Lily and Lorna* *The Pop Concert* *The Salt and Pepper Boys*

CAT'S WITCH
AND THE
MONSTER

KARA MAY

illustrated by Doffy Weir

TIGERS

Andersen Press·London

For Aylin

Text © 1992 by Kara May
Illustrations © 1992 by Doffy Weir

First published in 1992
by Andersen Press Limited,
20 Vauxhall Bridge Road, London SW1V 2SA.
This edition published 2002.

British Library Cataloguing in Publication Data available
ISBN 0 86264 379 1

Typesetting by Tek Art Limited, Croydon, Surrey
Printed and bound in China

1

Cat's Witch and the Monster

At the end of a bumpy little lane
was a little house. It was called
Roof Hole House after the hole in
its roof. In this house lived Cat
and his witch, Aggie.

5

At this moment, Cat was having a snooze. Aggie was sitting with her feet up on the fireplace, reading the *Witchety News*. She chanced to look round and out of the window.

'Oh no!' groaned Cat's witch Aggie. She groaned again, a very

loud groan that went whizzing
round the room, bounced off the
walls and jumped into the
fireplace, where it exploded with a

POP!

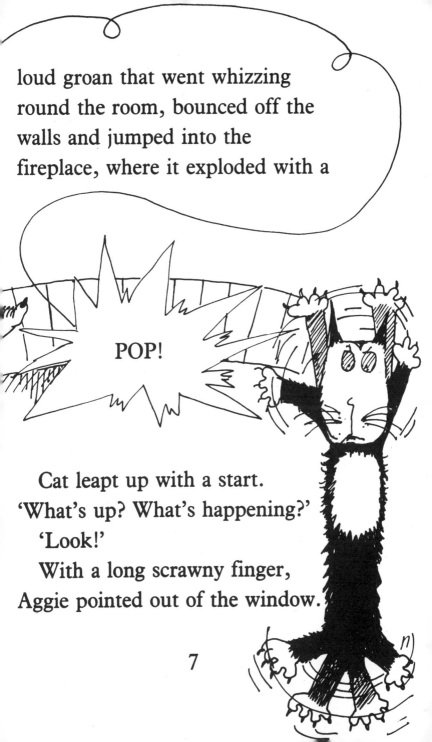

Cat leapt up with a start.
'What's up? What's happening?'
   'Look!'
With a long scrawny finger,
Aggie pointed out of the window.

7

Cat bristled. 'Aggie, how many times have I told you? Pointing is bad manners! Not sometimes. But always!'

Manners were important to Cat. How he wished his witch had more of them. How he wished his witch was more of a lady with a gentle voice and a polite way of behaving. But now he was curious to see what had upset her, and he leapt up onto the window-sill.

Coming down the road was a crowd of people led by the schoolteacher, Mr Smart, and Lucinda, a large white duck. They came from the town which was called Wantwich and the

people called themselves Wantwichers after it. It was a brand new town with a brand new park. In the centre of the park was a large lake, a very old lake and a very fine one. A large assortment of ducks and drakes lived there and people came from far and wide to admire them. Lucinda was the Head Duck.

'They've not come here for the exercise,' said Cat's witch Aggie. 'They're here because they want something.'

'If they want something that means money!' Cat shook the money box. It was almost empty.

'I'm not in the mood for working,' yawned Aggie.

'And I'm not in the mood for starving from hunger. Which is what we'll be doing if we don't get some money soon!'

'All right, all right, there's no need to go on.' Aggie went to the front door, and opened it. 'Well, what is it?' she bellowed at the crowd coming up the path.

'Manners,' muttered Cat.

'Manners.'

Aggie glared at him, then glared at the Wantwichers.

'Well, come on, I haven't got all day.'

'Aggie, dear, we need your help,' said Lucinda.

'Help costs money,' snapped Aggie.

'Oh we'll pay, of course we'll pay!' chorused the Wantwichers.

Aggie sighed, a long wheezy sigh. 'All right then, tell me what's the problem.'

Both Lucinda and Mr Smart began to talk at once. Aggie shut up Mr Smart with a look. 'You'll blither on for hours. Let the duck talk. Come on, quack it out, Lucinda.'

Cat shuddered and again muttered, 'Manners, Aggie, manners.'

But Lucinda went on, 'In a word, dear Aggie, it's the lake.'

'Yes, it's the lake,' repeated the Wantwichers.

'If you're all going to speak at once –' Aggie made towards the door. But Cat pulled her back. 'Oh no you don't. You stay and listen.' He bowed to Lucinda. 'Pray, do continue.'

'In a word, or rather five words, there's a monster in it,' said Lucinda.

Aggie's mouth dropped and
Cat's eyes popped. 'A monster in
the lake!' they cried. They hadn't
expected this!

'What sort of monster?' asked
Aggie.

'I haven't actually *seen* it. But I can feel it.' At the very thought, Lucinda began to shake.

'It's the truth, Aggie!' piped up little Ali Shah. 'There's a monster there all right. I went to the lake yesterday and you really can feel there's something lurking at the bottom. Something horrible and creepy and cruel. You can't blame the ducks for clearing out.'

'Clearing out to where?' asked Aggie.

'To the school playing fields,' said Mr Smart. 'You can't kick a ball on it for feathers. The sooner that monster's removed from the lake, the better.'

'We'd be ever so grateful, Aggie dear,' said Lucinda.

'"Dear" is the word. Removing monsters is an expensive business. And I don't know if I've got the time –'

'You do, and you have,' said Cat.

'Slave-driver,' mumbled Aggie.

But she whistled up the broomstick. 'Let's have a look at this monster. To the lake,' she commanded.

The lake was a murky grey. A
breeze shivered over its surface.
As they peered into the deep dark
depths, Cat felt the hair on his
back stand up on end. Aggie felt
a cold chill run down her spine.

There was nothing to be seen –
but something was there.

'Harum scarum, there's no
mistake! A monster lies within
this lake!' cried Cat's witch
Aggie.

She looked again, and then she
saw it. A huge thing, a scaly
thing, with gaping jaws and eyes
as red as fire that glowed up
through the water.

No wonder the ducks and drakes had been so afraid. No wonder they'd fled from the lake.

Aggie was sure of one thing: that a monster such as this would never be content to stay in the deep dark depths. It was only a matter of time before he'd rise up from the lake. And then, Wantwich beware!

'You will get rid of it for us, won't you dear Aggie?' begged the Head Duck Lucinda.

'Just leave it to me!' said Cat's witch Aggie.

2

Cat's Witch Goes to School

Cat was sitting by the fire, having a think. A whole week had gone by since Aggie had said she'd get rid of the monster. But so far she hadn't so much as opened her spellbook.

'I want to talk to you, Aggie,' he said as she came into the room.

Aggie tried to brush past. 'I can't stop now. I've got the washing-up to do.'

Cat gasped in astonishment. Aggie

21

never washed so much as a
teaspoon without being asked –
and then she'd carry on as if
she'd been asked to chop off her
head!

I know what this means!
thought Cat. She's trying to get
out of something she wants to do
even less than the washing-up!
And I've a good idea what it is!

He looked Aggie straight in the
eye. 'In case you've forgotten,
Aggie Witch, you're supposed to
be getting rid of a certain monster
in a certain lake not a million
miles from here!'

'Oh that! I'll get round to it,'
said Aggie.

'When?' demanded Cat.

'People are beginning to talk. They're beginning to say you can't do it!'

Aggie shrugged. 'Let them! It's nothing to me.'

'It's something to me. You mightn't have any pride, but I have. And the sooner we do it, the sooner we get paid. Come on, let's get started.'

Cat strode over to the bookshelf and took down the spellbook.

'You won't find any monster spells in there. If you *must* know,' went on Aggie, 'it's a Beginners' Spellbook. Monsters are in the Super Witch Spellbook.'

'Why didn't you say? We'll buy one. We can just about afford it.'

'You can't buy one.' Aggie spoke slowly, as if the words were being pulled out of her, painfully, like teeth. 'They *give* you one when you've passed your Super Witch exam. And I've never got round to taking it!'

Cat leapt up in a rage. 'Are you saying that I, Cat, am a *Beginner* witch's cat?'

'There's nothing wrong with being a Beginner witch,' snapped Aggie.

'Except that you can't get rid of the monster! You'll be a laughing stock. And so will I!' Cat pulled Aggie up from her chair. 'You're going to take the Super Witch exam.'

'But it takes forever!'

'Oh no it doesn't!'

He picked up the latest copy of the *Witchety News* and pointed to an advertisement:

BE A SUPER WITCH IN A WEEK

at the

SUPER WITCH CRAM SCHOOL.

Address: Star 101, The Milky Way.

'I'm too old to go back to school,' protested Aggie.

'You're never too old to learn,' said Cat.

The next thing Aggie knew she was flying at full speed towards the Milky Way, with Cat steering the broomstick.

'In case you get lost accidentally on purpose,' he told her.

The Cram School was a large white round building with a glass roof. There seemed to be no doors but as they got near, a door slid open. Cat pushed Aggie into the entrance hall.

Aggie sighed with relief. 'No one's here. Good. Come on, let's go.'

But at that moment a woman appeared out of the air before them. She wore high-heeled shoes

and a smart suit.
It was the Head,
Ms Emerald, so
called after her
hair which was a
brilliant green.
She looked Aggie
up and down as
if she was
something the
cat had brought
in – which
indeed she was.

29

Cat bowed with a smile that
Aggie thought was sickening but
which Cat thought was
gentlemanly.

'This is Aggie, Your Headness,
and I'm Cat. Aggie desires to
partake of the Super Witch
exam.'

'Does she indeed!' Ms Emerald turned to Aggie. 'It takes work. A lot of hard work. Are you sure you're up to it?'

Cat gave Aggie no chance to reply. 'She's as tough as old boots.'

'Mmm, we'll see. Come this way.'

They followed Ms Emerald down the long spotlessly clean corridor.

'In my day, schools were schools,' grumbled Aggie. 'Nice homely places with dust and lots of cobwebs.'

'One must move with the times,' said Ms Emerald.

'Why?' demanded Aggie.

Ms Emerald gave her an icy look as she pressed a button in the wall.

'This is the Cram Room,' she said.

Before them was a vast round room with a domed ceiling. There were long rows of computers with a witch in front of each one. Beside each witch was a robot.

'XRP, here's your witch for the week,' said Ms Emerald.

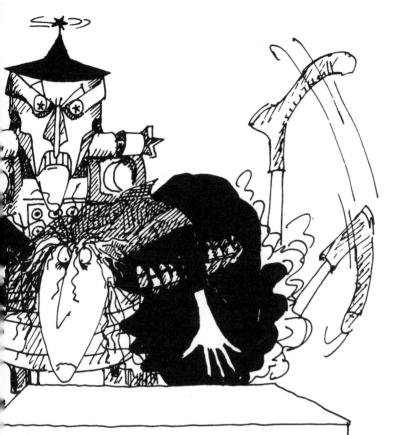

A robot with a stern, unsmiling face clanked across the room, picked up Aggie and plonked her in front of the computer. When Aggie looked round Cat and Ms Emerald had gone and the door had shut behind them.

'I-will-put-in-floppy-disc,' said XRP.

'What's a floppy disco when it's at home?'

XRP showed her a small plastic disc. He put it into the computer.

'Owls and asps! How about that!' cried Aggie, as words flashed onto the screen before her.

LESSON ONE
HOW TO MAKE YOURSELF INVISIBLE

1. Eat no food for one week beforehand.

2. Drink only one cup of water daily.

3. Take a bath every 4 hours.

Before Aggie had time to read
anymore, XRP commanded:
'Start learning.'

'I need a rest and a snack,'
said Aggie after about ten
minutes.

'Rest-hour-is-14-hours-to-15-
hours. Eat-hour-is-18-to-19-hours,'
XRP replied.

'This isn't a school!' squawked
Aggie. 'It's a torture chamber.'

She jumped up and ran to the door. Cat was sitting outside it.

'Back you go!' he snapped at her.

Every time Aggie tried to get out, Cat sent her back in.

XRP had taught many witches. But never, ever, had he taught a witch like Aggie.

'Slave-driver,' she screeched, when he asked her to recite her spells.

'I'm going on strike! I won't do it!' she said, when he told her to practise her wand-waving.

She moaned and she groaned and got into tempers and stormed about 'the torture chamber', as

she called it, till XRP threatened
to throw her out.

'You-have-one-more-chance-
Aggie-Witch. Either-stay-and-
behave-or-you-go-RIGHT-NOW.'

Aggie caught sight of Cat glowering at her through the door. 'You get to work or I leave you. Forever. And that's a promise,' he told her.

Aggie saw that he meant it. Still moaning and groaning but under her breath instead of at the top of her voice, she started to practise her wand-waving.

At last the week was up. Now the exam loomed before her.

'I'll take you to your exam cell. Follow me,' said Ms Emerald.

The cell was just big enough for a chair and a desk. On the desk was a pile of exam papers and an apple.

'Good luck, Aggie,' said Cat.

'She won't pass, she hasn't a chance,' sniffed Ms Emerald. 'I'll be back in the morning,' she added, as she locked the cell door behind her.

Aggie picked up the first exam paper. The words swam on the page. And when at last she could read the first questions, her heart sank.

QUESTION 1: How do you remove a wart from a weasel?

QUESTION 2: What wand-waves do you use to make the sun shine?

Her mind was a blank, there was nothing inside it.

'I'll fail the exam and Cat will leave me and the monster will eat the ducks and the drakes and the Wantwichers. And it will all be my fault because I couldn't get rid of it! Oh, was there ever such a woe-filled Aggie Witch?' wailed Cat's witch Aggie.

She looked at the questions again and as she looked, an answer glimmered.

She picked up her pen and started to write. And once she started, she didn't stop. The next thing she knew Ms Emerald was saying, 'Time's up. Hand in your answers.'

Aggie was so worn out she couldn't get up from her chair. When Cat asked her how she'd got on, she couldn't even speak.

'This-will-revive-you,' said XRP handing her a cup of Milky Way Special Brew.

By the time Ms Emerald came back with the results, Aggie was her old self again. She grinned, a large smirky grin. 'I've passed, haven't I?'

'Yes, I'm afraid you have!' said Ms Emerald. 'Here's your Super Witch Spellbook, your Super Witch Spoon and your Super Witch Wand.'

Aggie gave a shriek of excitement and pranced about yelling, 'What a clever little witch I am, I am!'

Cat looked on in embarrassment. 'I – er – think we'd better be going.'

With skirts flying, Aggie took a running jump onto the broomstick. 'Watch out, monster, here I come! It's Aggie Super Witch!'

'We-won't-see-like-of-her-again!' said XRP.

'I should hope not!' sniffed Ms Emerald as Cat and his witch vanished into the stars and headed back to Wantwich.

3

Cat Courageous

When they got back to Roof Hole House, Cat and his witch found a crowd gathered outside.

'We thought you'd done a flit, Aggie dear, and left us with the monster,' said Lucinda.

'So that's what you think of me!' Aggie was furious. 'If you knew the agony I've been through

to get a spell to help you! I've half
a mind not to bother.'

'Cut the cackle,' said Cat.
'Let's get on with it.'

Aggie was so thrilled at passing
her exam she wasn't in the mood
to argue. Carefully she opened
her new spellbook. The pages

were crisp and clean. It had been worth all she'd been through to get it, she thought. Not that she'd ever admit it to Cat.

'Here it is! This is the spell we want! Quiet everyone. I'll read it out,' said Cat's witch Aggie.

'SPELL FOR GETTING RID OF MONSTERS FROM LAKES

Spell Ingredients

1. One rowing boat.
2. One full moon.
3. One cat, with guitar.

Spell Method:

1. At midnight, when the moon is full, the cat must row the boat *alone* to the middle of the lake.

2. Then the cat must sing the monster-removal spell song whilst playing the guitar.

3. No matter what happens next, the cat must not return to shore till a nightingale sings.

WARNING: If the cat tries to return to shore before he/she hears the nightingale, the writer of this spell wouldn't like to say what will happen.'

A silence fell. For a full minute, no one spoke.

'We have a rowing boat on the lake,' Mr Smart said at last. 'We also have a full moon tonight.'

'And we've got lots of cats in Wantwich,' put in little Ali Shah.

Mr Smart nodded. 'But have

we got one with the courage for a job like this?'

'Only one way to find out,' said Aggie, 'and that's to ask. Come back when you've found one – *if* you find one!' she added.

The Wantwichers turned to troop off back into town.

'Wait! There's no need for that!'

Everyone looked round to see who had spoken.

'I'll do it,' said Cat.

Aggie turned suddenly pale. 'No, Cat. You can't. You mustn't. You might . . . ' her voice faded at the thought of what might happen to him.

Cat smiled gravely. 'I can and I must. You are a Super Witch, Aggie, and I am a Super Witch's Cat. No matter what befalls me it's my duty and I shall not flinch from it.'

'Oh I say, dear, how noble!' sighed Lucinda.

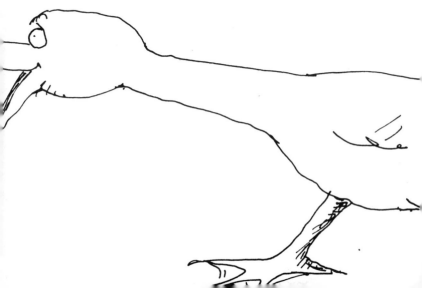

'You have our everlasting admiration and thanks,' said Mr Smart.

'I should think so too!' said Aggie. 'Now, clear off, let him get some rest.'

When they had gone Aggie, who hated cooking almost as much as she hated cleaning, cooked a huge dish of baked fish for Cat's dinner.

Cat pushed it away. 'Sorry, Aggie. Just don't feel hungry!'

'After all the trouble I've taken!' screeched Aggie. But she was instantly sorry. 'Oh Cat, forgive me. If I was going to do what you're going to do, I couldn't eat a mouthful either. Look,' she went on, 'I'll tell them you've changed your mind. It's

their monster. Let one of their cats get rid of it.'

Cat shook his head. 'No, Aggie. Wantwich is our town. These are our people, our ducks and drakes. It's up to us to help them.'

At last, midnight approached. Everyone gathered at the lake. They all shook hands with Cat. Aggie gave him a big hug. Her throat was so full of tears she couldn't say a word.

Cat pushed the boat away from the shore. As he rowed towards the middle of the lake, clouds blotted out the stars and moon. His heart was thumping so loudly he was sure the monster would hear it and be warned of his coming.

'I'm shaking so much,' he muttered, 'I can hardly hold the oars.'

But his pride was stronger than his fear. He picked up the guitar and began to sing in a voice that was weak and faint:

The stars are gone,
The moon has fled
And darkness fills the sky.
Oh Monster, rise from your watery bed,
There's no one here but I, but I,
There's no one here but I.

Now, Cat's voice grew a little stronger.

I sing a song that's strange but true
About an ancient King of Peru.
He rode on the back of a kangaroo
To the deepest depths of the ocean blue

And there he married a mermaid he
                                  knew
With his foot in his hat and his head in
                                  his shoe
That's what he did, the King of Peru.

Cat took a deep breath, and willed
his voice to ring strong and clear
across the lake.

I've sung my song, my song is sung,
Now heed this warning cry:
Oh Monster, flee from this lake
                              herewith –
Or sure as fate you die, you die, you
                                   die,
As sure as fate you die!

At that instant the wind
moaned and whipped across the
lake. The waves stirred and the
boat began to rock. Quickly Cat

reached for the oars. He was
about to head for shore when he
remembered he must wait for the
nightingale.

Silently he prayed, 'Please,
nightingale, sing!'

In reply came a roar of
thunder. A streak of lightning
shot across the sky and struck the
water. A pillar of flames spurted

high from the depths of the lake.
The waves rose up, lifting the
boat with it.

This is it, thought Cat. This is
the end. He would be thrown into
the water, the monster's prey.

He shut his eyes and waited.

But suddenly, all was still.
Across the lake came the song of
a bird. A nightingale was singing.

Cat looked round. The lake
was calm. The moon and stars
shone bright onto its smooth clear
water. Still trembling a little, he
picked up the oars and began to
row.

As he stepped ashore, the silence held. No one spoke for quite some time.

It was Aggie who spoke first. 'The monster has gone. Thanks to you, Cat,' she said simply.

Then a joyful shout went up: 'Hurrah for Cat.'

The next evening a party was held in thanks to Aggie and Cat.

'You're a Super Witch, Aggie,' said Cat.

'And you're a very Super Cat,' said Cat's witch Aggie.